Jacopo

DISCARD

by Linda Kay White

with illustrations by
AJ White

ISBN-10: 1479114529
ISBN-13: 9781479114528

Library of Congress Control Number: 2012915198
CreateSpace Independent Publishing Platform
North Charleston, South Carolina

Jacopo

by Linda Kay White

Linda Kay White

· Dedication ·

This book is dedicated to my husband, Larry, who requested that I write a children's story as his Christmas present. He is a pep squad, booster club, and fan club all rolled into one dear man.

It is also dedicated to our son, AJ, who not only produced illustrations to support the text at our request, but managed to consume copious cups of coffee, thereby supporting the production of the book and the coffee industry to boot!

Thanks to the support of my wonderful family, Jacopo has come to life.

· Chapter One ·

*in which we meet Jacopo the little monkey
and he gets his listening ears.*

The how and why of his name was a mystery to Jacopo, but to the little monkey, it didn't matter. He thought it was a very fine name.

Jacopo's earliest memory was of a soft and gentle voice.

"Now you hold still while I sew on your other ear, Jacopo. Whoever heard of a one-eared monkey? You do want to hear everything clearly, don't you?"

Oh, yes! Jacopo certainly did want to hear everything.

"There. That's much better. I always prefer speaking to firmly attached listening ears, don't you?"

Who was speaking to him? Jacopo thought for a moment. What exactly were listening ears, for that matter (firmly attached or not.)

But the voice continued, "You see, almost everybody has ears, but not all ears are firmly attached. I know that's true, because all too many people can only hear what they want to hear."

"Now, if you don't mind, these old eyes need to take a little break from sewing. So I'll just make myself a nice hot cup of tea, and then we'll decide what kind of eyes you should have. You'll like that, won't you, Jacopo?"

Gentle hands tucked Jacopo into a warm corner which began to rock back and forth. The movement gradually slowed to a stop. "What a very pleasant sensation," Jacopo thought to himself.

Curious about where he was and who had been speaking to him, Jacopo tingled all over. So he impatiently waited and listened, and the little monkey wondered just what he would see first.

· Chapter Two ·

~~~~~~

*in which Jacopo meets the kind lady
who spoke to him.*

The tea break ended, and Jacopo soon felt himself lifted out of the cozy corner where he had been left. Firm hands turned him this way and that.

"Now, what sort of eyes shall we give you, Jacopo?" asked the voice. "Should they be wise eyes, or maybe mischievous ones? I think they should be just curious enough to invite questions, but happy enough to reflect the friendly little monkey that you are, Jacopo."

Jacopo's ears perked up. He didn't remember very much, but surely he had always been a little monkey.

Hadn't he? Maybe he had or maybe not. Jacopo felt very confused.

Suddenly, a thin, shiny thing with a long black tail darted toward his face. It disappeared too quickly for him to make it out. "What was that? I saw something, but it's gone! What was it?"

Jacopo wanted to shout his questions out loud. He needn't have worried about not being able to make any sounds whatsoever yet. That was all right, because the familiar, reassuring voice quickly explained away all of his anxiety.

"There now, Jacopo. I know you only have one eye so far, but that's certainly better than none. Don't let this needle and thread frighten you. It doesn't hurt a bit, does it? Of course, it doesn't. I hope the sight of it whizzing around in front of your face didn't alarm you too much."

Then, as Jacopo listened intently, something wonderful happened. Above him, a face began to appear, set in concentration. Meanwhile, busy hands stitched his other eye into place.

A sudden tug knotted the thread, followed by a quick snip, and familiar hands lifted Jacopo into the air. From arms' length, he stared back into the friendliest face he had ever seen. Jacopo was thrilled.

· Chapter Three ·

*in which Jacopo gets a tail and
a terrible fright!*

The first face he ever saw was laced in fine lines. Glasses perched on the end of the nose, but such details went unnoticed by Jacopo. He was content just to finally look into the lady's eyes, and would have liked to savor the moment.

Alas, the moment passed all too quickly, because the lady had other plans. "Just as I thought," the lady declared cheerily. "Those eyes are the perfect complement to your ears. Now, let's add your tail."

With that, she dropped him unceremoniously onto his tummy. Staring at the floor, Jacopo wondered, "What's a tail?" He had no idea, but if the lady wanted to give him one, it must be useful.

Behind him, the silver needle flashed this way and that. The lady turned Jacopo first onto one side, then the other; and lastly, upside down. He felt the thread pulled tight and knotted. Then – snip! The lady laid aside her scissors, and Jacopo found himself gazing into her smile again.

"That's better, Jacopo. Did you wonder why it took me so long to get around to that important detail? Well, I wanted you to hear and see me before any mischievous thoughts got you into trouble."

"Whatever does she mean?" wondered Jacopo. "How would I get into mischief when I don't know what mischief is?"

Jacopo began to feel that his head was stuffed full of questions. But then, the lady rose from her chair. With Jacopo tucked under her arm, she walked a little unsteadily across the room and stopped before a large, shiny object on the wall.

The lady smiled deeply at him for a long moment, but with a small sigh, she turned him away from her gaze. Jacopo thought she sounded a little sad.

When Jacopo found himself looking at another lady in the shiny thing, all his previous thoughts vanished. That lady held in her hands another little monkey. How curious!

Jacopo had only heard one voice since getting his listening ears. He was very sure that no one else had come into the room. Who was staring back at him?

"See what a handsome fellow you are, Jacopo! Don't you agree?"

How, how could this be? The words Jacopo heard clearly came from the lady who held him. But it seemed as though the lady in front of him was speaking, too. Was this magic?

When Jacopo's lady turned him from side to side, the other lady copied her actions.

"Now, you have the perfect little monkey's tail, Jacopo. But don't you go getting yourself into trouble. No climbing up the lamps or drapes. Do you understand?"

"Do I understand?" wondered Jacopo. "I'm a monkey and I can both hear and see. What use there is for my new tail is bound to come to me. But who were that other lady and monkey?" These and other questions buzzed noisily around inside Jacopo's head.

Meanwhile, the lady carefully propped Jacopo in the corner of her chair. With a little push, she set it rocking. "That's enough sewing for today, Jacopo. You just sit here and rest a while. My garden wants some weeding today."

The lady stretched her back and crossed slowly to a coat rack near the door. Pausing to stroke the blossoms, she took down a straw hat blooming in silk flowers and put it on. She turned briefly to wink at Jacopo and went out the door.

Jacopo's chair did not face the door. Although he heard the door shut with a sharp click, Jacopo did not see someone (or something) slip inside before it closed. As the rocking chair gradually slowed to a stop, it now sat watching him.

"The lady will explain everything," Jacopo decided. All the questions buzzing around inside his tired head combined with the steadily ticking clock and gently rocking chair to make him very drowsy.

Suddenly, a pair of furry ears, followed by two amber eyes appeared over the edge of Jacopo's chair. His heart leapt and began beating wildly!

· Chapter Four ·

*in which Jacopo fears
he will be eaten by a beast.*

Immediately following the furry ears and amber eyes came a pink nose flanked on either side by enormously long white whiskers. Had he known how, Jacopo would have jumped up and scrambled to the top of the tallest thing in the room, a bookcase stretching almost to the ceiling.

The lady's eyes were blue not amber, and she definitely did not have pointed, furry ears. Even if the lady and her monkey from the shiny object on the wall had somehow escaped and made their way to where Jacopo sat, he would have recognized them. Who or what was this?

Then an orange, furry body followed the ears, eyes, nose, and whiskers as it leapt into Jacopo's chair. A furry paw patted Jacopo's chest as he sat trembling in fear. When it leaned even closer to delicately sniff him all over, Jacopo could feel its warm breath.

"I'm to be eaten by a wild beast," Jacopo thought grimly. "The kind lady will find nothing left of me but a few scraps."

"Don't be ridiculous," a voice said. Where did it come from? "I have no intention of eating you." With that, the beast closed its eyes, turned around once, and flopped down with its head upon its paws.

"Are you talking to me?" Jacopo wondered to himself. Since his mouth was not finished yet, he couldn't very well ask out loud.

The beast opened one eye and peered at Jacopo. "Of course I'm speaking to you," it replied with a sigh and shut its eye again.

Then the beast began to rumble inside, vibrating through the chair's cushion, all the way down to the end of Jacopo's tail and tips of his toes. Jacopo trembled even harder, and he nearly fainted away when the beast yawned, displaying some very, very sharp teeth.

This time, the beast didn't bother to open even one eye. "This is called purring. If you knew anything, you would know that purring is a very good sign, not something to be afraid of. You would also know that I only eat fish." The beast paused. "I eat fish and the occasional mouse or bird, if I'm lucky."

The beast suddenly opened both eyes, sat up on its haunches, and stared deeply into Jacopo's eyes.

"Why do you think I smelled you all over? To see if you were worth eating, of course."

Then the beast turned its back to Jacopo, flopped down again with its head resting on Jacopo's legs, and purred even more loudly. Except for occasionally twitching its magnificent tail, the beast did not move again.

Jacopo began to relax a little. Even the loud purring seemed less scary, and Jacopo found that he rather enjoyed the warm body next to his. It reminded him of sitting in the lady's lap as she worked on him.

The beast's tail twitched in rhythm with the ticking clock. "What a clever tail the beast has," Jacopo thought to himself.

Jacopo's tail lay curled up beside him. He tried to imagine himself wearing the beast's beautiful furry tail. Finally, he decided, "The lady herself chose this tail for me and sewed it on. I'm sure it is the tail that suits me best."

He examined the beast's ears, too, and compared them to his own. "I wonder if being pointed makes them better for listening."

Jacopo remembered the long white hairs on each side of the beast's nose. "They look very elegant. What are they for, and will the lady give me long white hairs, too?"

No sooner had Jacopo recovered from his beastly encounter, than the door opened once more. The lady had returned. "What's all this?" she exclaimed.

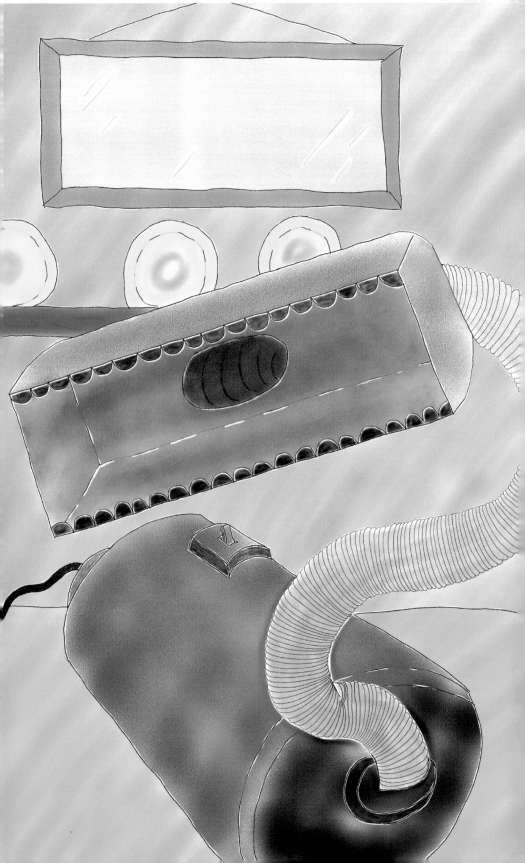

· Chapter Five ·

in which Jacopo encounters another beast!

The lady removed her hat and gloves as she reentered the room. Tossing them aside, she made straight for Jacopo's chair. Unconcerned, the beast slept on.

"Tsk, tsk, tsk, Catapus," the lady scolded, as without a pause, she scooped the beast up and carried him like a sack of potatoes straight back to the door.

Jacopo spied the beast winking slyly as he was dumped unceremoniously on the front stoop. "This is a little game we play, Jacopo," he heard the beast say. "She always throws me out, and I always sneak back in. You're in my chair. Remember that it's my chair. I'll be back for it!"

The lady closed the door firmly, shutting out any further comments from Catapus. Then she dusted her hands together and marched straight back to where Jacopo sat trying to understand what had so upset the lady.

In a very businesslike way, she whisked Jacopo out of the chair and examined him up and down. "No, no, no," she grumbled to herself. "This will never do. Not even finished yet, and already covered in cat fur. Well, I'll soon take care of that."

She dropped Jacopo into the chair, where he landed on his tummy in a very undignified position, his face buried in the chair's cushion. Jacopo lay there as she marched out of the room, trying to understand why the lady was so displeased with him.

He did not have long to wait. ROARRRR! A loud noise was coming closer and closer. Jacopo had a terrible thought; maybe there was more than one beast in the lady's house.

That terrible thought was replaced by something even worse. What if it was a hungrier beast that did want to gobble him up? Jacopo felt as though he would melt right through the chair's cushion and into the floor below.

When the lady came into the room with the very beast that was making such horrible noises, some of Jacopo's fear was replaced by confusion. He felt himself snatched out of the chair and held face to face with the lady who didn't look angry or frightened. In fact, she was smiling!

The lady attempted to reassure Jacopo that he was not going to be eaten, but Jacopo, positive that the end had come, resigned himself to fate. If only he could shut out whatever was about to happen by squeezing his eyes tightly closed.

A frightened Jacopo heard air rushing into the gaping jaws of the beast as it snaked closer and closer. Then, the roaring, eyeless thing lunged at Jacopo, and attacked him from head to foot while the lady held him in a no-nonsense grip.

· Chapter Six ·

in which Jacopo, fortunately, survives an attack.

J acopo knew that he would be swallowed up whole any second now. But to his very great delight, when the howling thing attacked his legs, tummy, back, even his tail and head, the lady easily pulled him free.

To his immense relief, the attacks didn't hurt Jacopo one little bit. Despite the fearsome noises coming out of the monster, Jacopo could see that there wasn't a single tooth in its mouth.

The lady dropped the monster, and with a flourish of her hand, flipped a switch on its body. Was the monster dead? Had she killed it?

The lady carefully examined the confused and exhausted little monkey, turning him over, around, and upside down. Apparently satisfied, she brought him up face to face with herself, smiled, and nodded.

"There, Jacopo. I do believe we have succeeded in removing all that kitty fur. Catapus is really the cleverest cat I've ever seen in all my days. Honestly, I do not know how he manages to slip in here."

After first brushing away a few stray cat hairs, the lady sat down in the chair with Jacopo on her lap.

"Did you think, Jacopo, that my vacuum cleaner was some great beast about to swallow you whole? I probably should have explained it to you first. Well, no harm done," the lady chuckled.

No harm done? "I've been frightened nearly out of my wits," thought Jacopo, "and barely escaped being eaten alive. No harm done?" Jacopo couldn't believe his ears. How could she laugh about it?

But gazing up into the lady's kind eyes, and feeling how gently she held him, Jacopo could not be angry with her. He knew now that what happened to him had been done for his own good, without malice.

"We live in a big, wide world, Jacopo. There are a great many more lessons ahead of you, I fear, but you are a clever little monkey. I am confident that you will learn *and remember* your lessons well."

Jacopo did want to learn everything he could, and so he listened carefully to the lady's words. After all, she had explained about the cat and the vacuum cleaner. He would try his very best to make her happy.

The lady seemed to remember the reason why she had returned to Jacopo in the first place before finding him covered in cat fur.

"Now, it is high time we gave some thought to your costume, Jacopo." She looked across the room at her straw hat, and smiled. "I'm quite partial to hats myself."

Jacopo remembered the lady's straw hat and that she seemed very fond of it.

Turning him this way and that, she continued speaking more to herself than to Jacopo. "Yes, we definitely will begin with your hat, considering your lovely ears . . ."

Instantly, Jacopo's ears perked up. "What about my ears?"

But the lady did not explain. Instead, she pulled herself to her feet and tucked him back into the chair. As she walked away, Jacopo heard the lady wondering aloud, "Now where did I put that black tassel?"

· Chapter Seven ·

in which Jacopo gets a new hat and learns that everything is not what it seems.

When the lady returned, she carried not only the black tassel, but also red fabric, brown paper, scissors, thread, and a pincushion bristling with pins and needles.

Instead of joining Jacopo in their chair as he expected, the lady carried her armload to a table on the other side of the room. Dumping everything on the table, she sat down, pushed the pile to one side, and drew the brown paper toward her.

Then she hoisted herself back up again muttering, "Now why didn't I bring a pencil, too?"

Passing him on her way back to the table with the found pencil, she paused to waggle her finger at Jacopo. "It's your fault, you know. Why didn't you remind me that I needed a pencil to draw the pattern for your new hat?" Then she winked, and continued on her way.

Her question puzzled Jacopo. "How could I know that she would need a pencil? I don't even know what a pencil is," he wondered.

"But she did wink at me. Maybe she was making a little joke."

Relieved, Jacopo waited for the lady to finish her work. He entertained himself with his new memories. So much had happened to Jacopo since he first got his ears and heard the lady's voice.

Jacopo remembered how nice it felt to rock back and forth in the chair. Then, he remembered his fright when Catapus jumped into his chair, and how surprised he was to learn that the beast was only a cat.

Jacopo had just begun to remember the vacuum cleaner-beast, when something else occurred to him. Catapus had been able to read Jacopo's thoughts, but he could not read the cat's.

He wondered, "Can the lady read my thoughts, too?" Jacopo didn't think so. He knew that he couldn't read hers.

Time passed pleasantly. The lady continued with sewing for two whole hours, while Jacopo tried to solve his puzzles. He heard paper rustling and scissors snipping, and nicest of all, the lady humming softly as she worked.

When she finally rose from the table and made her way across the room to him, Jacopo was surprised to see darkened windows.

The lady carried something red with a black tail in her hands. As she walked, the tail swung gently to and fro. "Did she make another monkey?" he wondered.

"Now, Jacopo, let's see how you like your new hat." She settled into the chair with Jacopo on her lap. As they rocked back and forth, she positioned the new hat on his head, tilting it right, left, backward, and forward. Eventually, she perched it exactly on the center of his head.

The black tail thing swung past his ears, first on one side, then on the other as she made her adjustments. "Oooooh, that tickles," thought Jacopo. "I feel wiggly all over!"

Satisfied at last, the lady began pinning the new hat to Jacopo's head. Since he had already learned that the lady's pins and needles didn't hurt, he didn't mind at all.

"I am stitching your new hat on, because a curious little monkey like you might easily lose it swinging through the branches outside, or even scampering up the bookcase over there during a game of hide and seek with Catapus," she explained to Jacopo as she sewed.

"Isn't that so, Jacopo?" She knotted the thread and snipped it with her scissors. Then she held him up, and looked directly into Jacopo's eyes.

"Maybe she can read my thoughts after all," thought Jacopo. "Maybe she'll answer me right now, and prove it." Instead, the lady merely tilted her head to one side.

Tucking Jacopo under her arm, she pulled herself out of the chair and shuffled across the room, where she stopped. She held Jacopo up to look into his face once more, and nodded. Then she spun him around.

He found himself gazing at the other lady again. And now she was holding the other monkey, who also was wearing a red hat with a black tail on his head.

"This is so very strange," thought Jacopo. "Why does she keep on making me look at that other lady and her monkey?"

"Look, Jacopo, what do you think of your new hat? It's called a fez. See how neatly it fits right between your wonderful ears? Does the tassel tickle them a little?"

The lady turned Jacopo from side to side as she spoke. The other lady and her monkey did exactly the same thing. Finally, the lady stopped turning Jacopo and held him so that he stared directly into the other monkey's eyes.

The lady traced her finger across some stitches on the front of the hat. "See, Jacopo? I've embroidered your name on your new hat. Even though the mirror turns it around backwards, your hat will say 'Jacopo' to everyone you meet."

She chuckled slightly then. "I just thought of the funniest thing, Jacopo. I never explained the mirror to you before. Did you think that you were looking at another monkey? Were you surprised?"

"Anyway," she said as she crossed the room and tucked Jacopo back into the rocking chair. "There's just us, Jacopo. You, me, and Catapus."

Planting her hands on her hips and tilting her head to one side, she winked. "But I think that's quite enough for today, don't you? Good night, Jacopo."

And with that, she gave the chair a little push to set it rocking, turned out the light, and slowly climbed the stairs to bed.

· Chapter Eight ·

in which Jacopo receives some grand new finery.

In the following days, Jacopo experienced one surprise after another as the lady fussed about with her pencil, brown paper, and pins.

Again and again, she stopped to sweep Jacopo up from his chair. Then the lady would pin him inside oddly shaped brown paper packages. Although bits of him (like his tail) stuck out, Jacopo wondered if the lady would wrap him up forever, tail and all.

Jacopo enjoyed the lady's company, and didn't mind being continually wrapped and unwrapped. Eventually, she replaced the crinkly brown wrapping paper with buttery soft leather. Jacopo liked how it felt and was a little disappointed when the lady removed those wrappings, too, and returned Jacopo to his chair.

From where he sat, Jacopo couldn't see everything that the lady did at her table. He could hear scissors snipping away and the lady humming over her work; that made him happy enough.

After endless fittings, she dressed him in his new clothing and Jacopo could tell that the lady was satisfied at last.

"Oh, Jacopo," she breathed softly. "Even if I do say so myself, you look very grand. Would you like a little peek?"

With Jacopo *(bursting with curiosity)* in the crook of her arm, the lady hoisted herself up out of the chair and made her way over to the mirror.

This time, Jacopo knew exactly who he saw in the mirror. As he and the lady peered at themselves, Jacopo was immensely pleased. He saw a very happy little monkey named Jacopo wearing a beautiful red fez, moss-colored lederhosen, and braid-trimmed suspenders.

As the lady turned him this way and that, Jacopo spied some little flowers, hearts, and fancy buttons decorating his new clothes. There were even some stitches in gold thread.

The lady whispered in his ear (*the one that was not being tickled by the tassel*), "Do you like your new clothes, Jacopo? I hope so, because they make you very handsome." Jacopo wished more than anything that he could tell the lady how grand they were.

"I think that will do for today," said the lady, carrying him back to the rocking chair. "Tomorrow, I intend to make sure your feet stay warm. The weather has been nippy lately. I don't want you to catch cold."

Then she tucked him into her chair, patted him lightly on the arm, winked, and turned out the light.

"Good night, Jacopo," she said, as she set the chair rocking with a gentle push. Then she slowly crossed the room and climbed the stairs up to bed.

As Jacopo slowly rocked, he admired his wonderful new clothes in the faint light of the glowing fireplace embers and thought about how happy he was to be living with the kind lady in this cozy house.

· Chapter Nine ·

*in which Jacopo receives a wonderful gift
and some terrible news.*

The next day, true to her word, the lady wrapped, unwrapped, pinned, and unpinned Jacopo's feet first into the familiar crinkly brown paper, and then into soft brown leather that matched his suspenders.

Jacopo didn't mind, because the lady talked to him about many things while she worked. He listened carefully to every word. Sometimes, he would have liked to ask her a question, but mostly he was content just to listen.

The lady took occasional breaks from her labors as the hours stretched on. That was fine with Jacopo, because it gave him time to turn his lessons over and over in his mind.

When his feet had been fitted into the new boots for the last time and securely stitched in place so they *(like the red fez)* could not be lost, Jacopo could only gaze in wonder. Turning his feet from side to side, the lady admired her handiwork.

His soft brown leather boots turned up at the toes, tipped by tiny brass bells. Topping off the boots, pointed moss-green leather cuffs held in place by brass buttons, also sported tiny bells.

Even if he had been able to speak, Jacopo could not have found the words to express his delight. Surely, in the entire world, no other monkey wore such finery!

Holding him up before her face, the lady smiled broadly into his eyes. "You are nearly finished, Jacopo."

Threading her needle, she delicately stitched on Jacopo's face. "With your listening ears, you can hear.

With your watching eyes, you can see. Your grand tail will help keep you out of danger, provided you are prudent in its use. The last gift I can give to you is a speaking mouth."

Time stood still. More than anything in the world, Jacopo wanted the ability to speak. Finally, he might be able to ask the questions that filled his head. Couldn't the lady stitch any faster?

The lady then offered Jacopo her final words of advice. "Before I tie this last knot and cut my thread, you must listen carefully since your very life may depend on it. Speech is a special gift. No matter how strong the urge to speak, you must restrain yourself, Jacopo."

The lady snipped her thread. Laying the sewing things aside, she gathered Jacopo into her arms, holding him close as if he were a real child.

"You are very special, and I will always love you, Jacopo. I know you will be very, very happy, but I already miss you most terribly."

"This is how love feels," Jacopo thought, feeling warmth spread throughout his cloth body.

He saw the lady's eyes glistening behind her glasses as she tenderly arranged him in her rocking chair. She slowly straightened herself and said, "I think you might like some company on this very cold night." Jacopo was worried at the loneliness in her voice.

The lady walked heavily to the door and opened it slightly. Catapus swept in on a gust of cold air. He meowed loudly several times, and then began purring as he rubbed himself around and around her legs.

Planting her fists firmly on her hips, the lady spoke sternly. "Now, Catapus, I am going to break one of my own rules tonight. Promise me faithfully that if I allow you to sleep indoors near the fire, you will not curl up in Jacopo's lap. Absolutely no leaving him covered in your kitty fur."

Jacopo detected the glimmer of mischief in the lady's eyes.

Her warning didn't seem to concern Catapus in the least. Twitching his tail haughtily, he bounded across the room and leapt onto the footstool in front of Jacopo.

The lady followed along more slowly. She stroked Catapus once or twice and scratched him under the chin. "There's a good kitty, Catapus."

Then she turned once more to Jacopo. "Tonight, you and Catapus keep each other company," she said. "You have lots to talk about, I'm sure. Good night, my friends."

The lady nodded at Jacopo before she set the chair to rocking and turned out the light. Listening to the lady's steps as she climbed slowly up the stairs, Jacopo fought back the urge to call out to her.

For a little while, the only sounds in the room came from the chair still slowly rocking back and forth, from the ticking clock, and from the snapping, popping fireplace embers. As Jacopo sat trying to understand everything, Catapus' loud purring suddenly stopped.

The cat sat up to address him. "Well, Jacopo, are you ready for your very last lesson before leaving here?"

· Chapter Ten ·

in which Jacopo speaks his first words and more besides.

Jacopo wanted to shout. "Leaving here? What do you mean, Catapus?" Was that what the lady meant when she whispered that she would miss him? Panic rose in Jacopo's chest. He didn't want to leave the lady's house. He wanted to stay here forever and ever with Catapus and the lady.

Catapus leaned toward Jacopo, and, lightly as a feather, tapped Jacopo's paw. Amber eyes gazed intently into Jacopo's. The cat's warm breath swirled about Jacopo's face.

"I know that you have a great many questions to ask, Jacopo. Now is the time for you to ask them."

"What about the lady?" Jacopo worried. "She said I must be very, very careful before speaking out loud."

Swinging his head from side to side, Catapus flicked his tail impatiently. "Believe me when I say that the lady has chosen not to hear either of us, Jacopo. Not even the tiniest scrap of our conversation could slip under her bedroom door; it is shut so tightly."

Jacopo couldn't believe his ears. Catapus was actually encouraging him to speak aloud! Continuing to stare into Jacopo's eyes, Catapus simply nodded.

Jacopo gingerly tried to move his lips. To his delight, his mouth opened. At first, he could only open and close it again and again. For a little while, he forgot all about speaking.

"You see, Jacopo? It's true. Thanks to the lady, you now have the ability to speak." Catapus smiled encouragingly. Jacopo tried to speak, but the sound of his own voice so shocked him that his mouth snapped shut again.

"Did that come out of me?" Jacopo wanted to know. "It's not what I expected to sound like at all." After waiting so long to ask so many questions, now he was too frightened of the sound of his own voice to speak!

"It's a big shock, I know, Jacopo, but that's all right. Do try again. Believe me, tonight no one will overhear what we say." Once more, Catapus patted Jacopo's paw.

When Jacopo did try again, he succeeded in getting out one question right after the other.

"What's happening, Catapus? Why will the lady miss me? Is she sending me away? Why? Did I do something terrible?"

"Calm yourself, Jacopo," purred Catapus. "You have nothing to be afraid of. All is as it must be. You were expressly made by the lady for the purpose of sharing grand adventures with a real person."

"What adventures? Why can't I share them with her? Catapus, I only know you and the lady. Who else is there?"

Jacopo paused as a new possibility crept into his mind. Maybe he would go adventuring with Catapus. That wouldn't be so bad. Now that he knew Catapus wasn't going to eat him, Jacopo had begun to think of Catapus as quite friendly.

"Is that it, Catapus?" he asked hopefully. "Is that what you mean?"

Catapus sighed and swung his head from side to side. He took a deep breath and continued. "No, Jacopo. I am a cat, not a person, and the lady is too old to go adventuring with you."

"You have yet to meet this special person, but very soon, you shall. That meeting will only be the beginning of many exciting adventures and a very special bond." He paused to draw himself up very tall. "I promise you this on my word as Catapus."

Catapus' words both thrilled and worried Jacopo. He still could not understand why he must leave.

Before Jacopo could ask any more questions, Catapus raised his paw and continued. "Tonight, I will be your teacher, so pay attention, Jacopo."

· Chapter Eleven ·

~~~~~~~~~~~~~~~~~~~~~~~~

in which Jacopo begins his lessons with Catapus.

"You have listened well, Jacopo. So far, you haven't broken any rules, but you must continue to practice restraint. It will be an even more difficult task tonight."

Then Catapus leapt out of the chair onto the floor. There he sat, staring expectantly at Jacopo.

The cat's sudden movement unnerved Jacopo. He didn't know which was racing faster, his head or his heart. What did Catapus expect? The little monkey didn't have to wait long for an answer.

"You can hear, see, and speak, Jacopo," purred Catapus. "Now, it is time for you to move."

"You want me to move?" *(Jacopo couldn't believe his ears.)*

Catapus nodded. "Start small. Turn your head from side to side, like this." The cat demonstrated by moving his head, his amber eyes never leaving Jacopo's.

Trapped in Catapus' gaze, unaware even of doing it, Jacopo swung his head side to side.

"That was amazing!" The words burst out of him. Jacopo clapped one paw over his mouth.

Catapus' eyes widened. "Perhaps this lesson will go a little faster than I anticipated."

Jacopo couldn't help himself as he giggled nervously behind his paw.

Catapus purred proudly, "You've come this far, Jacopo. You might as well move those legs of yours."

With surprise, Jacopo saw his legs lift and his knees bend, simply because he wished it. Impatiently, he asked, "What now, Catapus? What shall I do now?"

Catapus flicked his tail, sweeping it several times over the floor. "What do you think is next, Jacopo?" he asked slyly.

Jacopo caught the cat's hint, and watched his own tail curl up over the chair arm. "Can it do anything else?" He remembered what the lady had warned him about. "The lady told me not to use it for climbing the lamps or drapes."

"You were right to listen and not use it sooner. But I think the time has come for you to discover just how useful that tail of yours really is. I want you to join me down here, Jacopo."

With no further prompting, Jacopo scampered first to the ottoman, then back to the chair and onto its high back, gripping it with the aid of his clever tail.

The chair rocked rapidly back and forth with Jacopo perched atop the back. He balanced there, admiring the tinkling bells on his boots, and grinned broadly down at Catapus.

Catapus shook his head, "I asked you to join me down here, Jacopo. Have you already forgotten your lessons?"

Jacopo quickly scampered down onto the floor. He hung his head sheepishly and apologized to Catapus.

"I'm very sorry, Catapus. I will follow all of your other instructions very carefully." Still, he couldn't help smiling a little. "That felt wonderful! Did you hear the little bells? What shall we do now?"

"Patience, Jacopo." Catapus stifled his own smile. "Yes, I heard the little bells, but we cats are not so fond of bells as you monkeys. It interferes with our hunting. But, never mind about that. There is more ahead tonight than you could possibly imagine."

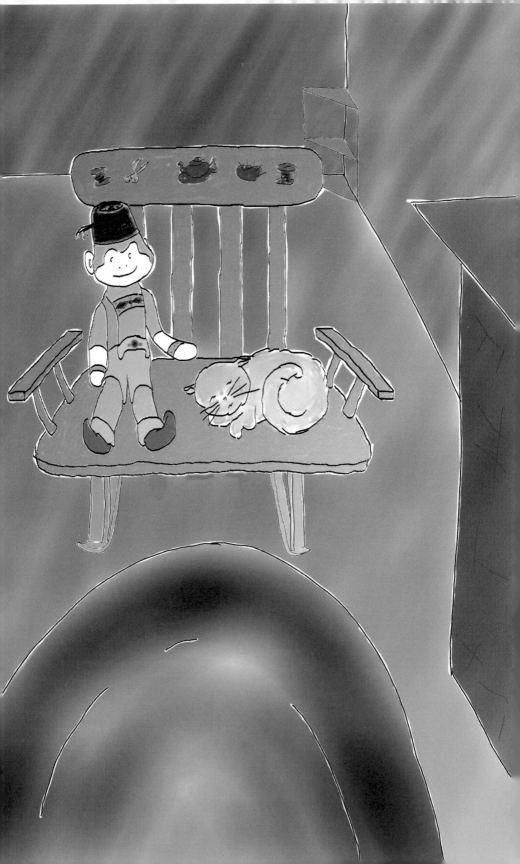

· Chapter Twelve ·

in which Jacopo must say goodbye to his friend Catapus.

Catapus was true to his word. The two friends played many games of Hide and Seek, Tag, and Statues, long after the last fireplace ember had died away. Jacopo did not realize it, but these exercises were not games. They were serious lessons that would serve Jacopo well when he left the lady's house.

Finally they were too exhausted to play any longer. Catapus suddenly sat down and turned to the little monkey with a stern expression. Skidding to a nose-to-nose stop, Jacopo searched the cat's face.

"What is it, Catapus?" He glanced over his shoulder at the darkened stairway. "Have we been too loud? Did we wake the lady?"

Catapus replied, "No, Jacopo. Remember how I told you that tonight the lady would not hear us? The time has come to cease playing. You must return to the same position in which she left you in her chair."

Suddenly, Catapus looked so very sad. More than anything, Jacopo wanted to comfort his friend. He longed to rub Catapus' fur and tickle him under the chin as he had seen the lady do. He also knew that the lady would be very upset if she found him covered in fur again.

Jacopo climbed dutifully back into the rocking chair, arranging himself exactly as he had been left. Catapus followed him and sat on the footstool facing Jacopo.

"Jacopo, there are no more lessons for me to teach you. You will fall asleep tonight, just as the lady and I do every night. But you will awaken to the beginning of many exciting adventures in a new house. Until then, you must neither move nor speak in the presence of humans."

As growing fear crept into Jacopo's heart, Catapus continued, "Do not be afraid, Jacopo. You have learned well and earned a happy life with your new companion. I promise that you will know when it is the right time for you to move and speak again."

"Will I ever see you or the lady again, Catapus?" Jacopo asked.

"Although you probably will not see the lady again, just remember this: she is as much a part of you as your ears or your tail," Catapus replied.

"As for me, I have enjoyed getting to know you, Jacopo." Then he winked slyly. "Everyone knows that a cat has nine lives. Who knows whether I might not cross paths with a certain little monkey in one of the other eight?"

Jacopo had been listening intently to Catapus, unaware that he had leaned so closely that they sat nearly nose-to-nose. He gently patted the cat's paw. "Catapus, my most excellent companion, the knowledge that I will never forget you or the lady makes me so very happy."

He paused, and then asked, "Will you try to remember me, too, please?"

Catapus cleared his throat before replying, and the cat's voice was a little gruffer than usual when he answered. "Never fear, Jacopo. I will most certainly remember you, too." Then, drawing himself up taller, Catapus announced, "It's time to sleep now, Jacopo. Good night, and happy adventuring, my little friend."

Settling back into the chair, Jacopo nodded. "Good night to you, too, my dear, dear friend," he whispered. Then Jacopo sat absolutely, perfectly still, leaving Catapus alone in the room.

There was only a ticking clock, a purring cat, and a toy monkey named Jacopo.

· Epilogue ·

When Jacopo next awoke, he was in his new surroundings. Sparkling green eyes framed in freckles gazed down at him from a cloud of red hair. The little girl in whose arms Jacopo awoke squeezed him tightly. She whispered, tickling his ears with these magic words, "Hello, Jacopo. My name is Jonelle. Would you like to visit my tree house?"

And so began Jacopo's many adventures with Jonelle, but that is a story for another time.

· Acknowledgement ·

I would be remiss if I did not thank my workmate at the Santa Cruz Public Library System, Leslie Auerbach, for all her enthusiastic support and meticulous proofreading skills. Thanks so much for never losing faith in me.

This is the original Jacopo, handmade by Linda K. White.

Yes, he really does exist.